From 1795 to 1845 **John Chapman**, better known as Johnny Appleseed, traveled through several states planting apple seeds.

Daniel Boone was born in Pennsylvania in 1734. He was one of the most famous frontiersmen in U.S. history.

Walt Whitman was an American poet. His most famous work is *Leaves of Grass*, which he self-published in 1855.

Sally Ride was the first American woman to travel in space. In 1987 she resigned from the astronaut program to become a professor.

Do YOU Have a Hat?

by Eileen Spinelli

illustrated by Geraldo Valério

SIMON & SCHUSTER BOOKS FOR YOUNG READERS

NEW YORK   LONDON   TORONTO   SYDNEY

SIMON & SCHUSTER BOOKS FOR YOUNG READERS
An imprint of Simon & Schuster Children's Publishing Division
1230 Avenue of the Americas, New York, New York 10020
Text copyright © 2004 by Eileen Spinelli
Illustrations copyright © 2004 by Geraldo Valério

SIMON & SCHUSTER BOOKS FOR YOUNG READERS is a trademark of Simon & Schuster, Inc.
Book design by Dan Potash
The text for this book is set in Mrs. Eaves. · The illustrations for this book are rendered in acrylic.
Manufactured in China
2 4 6 8 10 9 7 5 3 1
Library of Congress Cataloging-in-Publication Data
Spinelli, Eileen. · Do you have a hat? / Eileen Spinelli ; illustrated by Geraldo Valério. — 1st ed. · p. cm. · Summary: Rhyming text describes a great
variety of hats worn by celebrities throughout history. · ISBN 0-689-86253-9 · [1. Hats—Fiction. 2. Celebrities—Fiction. 3. Stories in rhyme.]
I. Valério, Geraldo, ill. II. Title. · PZ8.3.S759Do 2004 · [E]—dc22   2004007428

For Sue Shaw, Jean Soule, and Doris Markley.
And for Mary Lou Carney, Queen of Hats—E. S.

For Craig—G. V.

Do **YOU** have a hat?

Something fuzzy, warm, and red,
to keep the snowflakes off your head?

Or maybe floppy-brimmed and blue,
when summer sun shines down on you?

Do **YOU** have a hat?

Francisco de Goya had a hat,
a hat with candles on the brim—
a clever hat that suited him—
that made a chandelier of light
for painting far into the night.

Do YOU have a hat?

Igor Stravinsky had a hat,
a tattered, battered green beret.
He wore it every single day.
They say it never left his head—
not even when he went to bed!

Do **YOU** have a hat?

Carmen Miranda had a hat,
a towering hat of plums and cherries,
peaches, oranges, and berries,
plump bananas by the bunch—
a hat her friends could eat for lunch.

Do **YOU** have a hat?

Abraham Lincoln had a hat,
a stovepipe hat—black and tall—
a presidential carryall.

Abe Lincoln wore it round the town
with documents inside the crown.

Do **YOU** have a hat?

Nat Love had a hat,
a cowboy hat—to wear, of course,
or carry water to his horse,
to give a pesky fly a slap,
or play the pillow for his nap.
Do **YOU** have a hat?

Isabelle of Bavaria had a hat,
a cone-shaped hat so very high
it poked a gargoyle in the eye.
The doorways had to be redone
so she could fit through every one.

Do **YOU** have a hat?

Walt Whitman had a hat,
a rather old and shabby hat—
at times, a makeshift table mat—
for writing poems in the sun,
or eating supper on the run.

Do **YOU** have a hat?

Louis Comte had a hat,
a hat to close his magic act.
A normal-looking hat, in fact.
But reaching in—as was his habit—
Louis produced a bunny rabbit.

Do **YOU** have a hat?

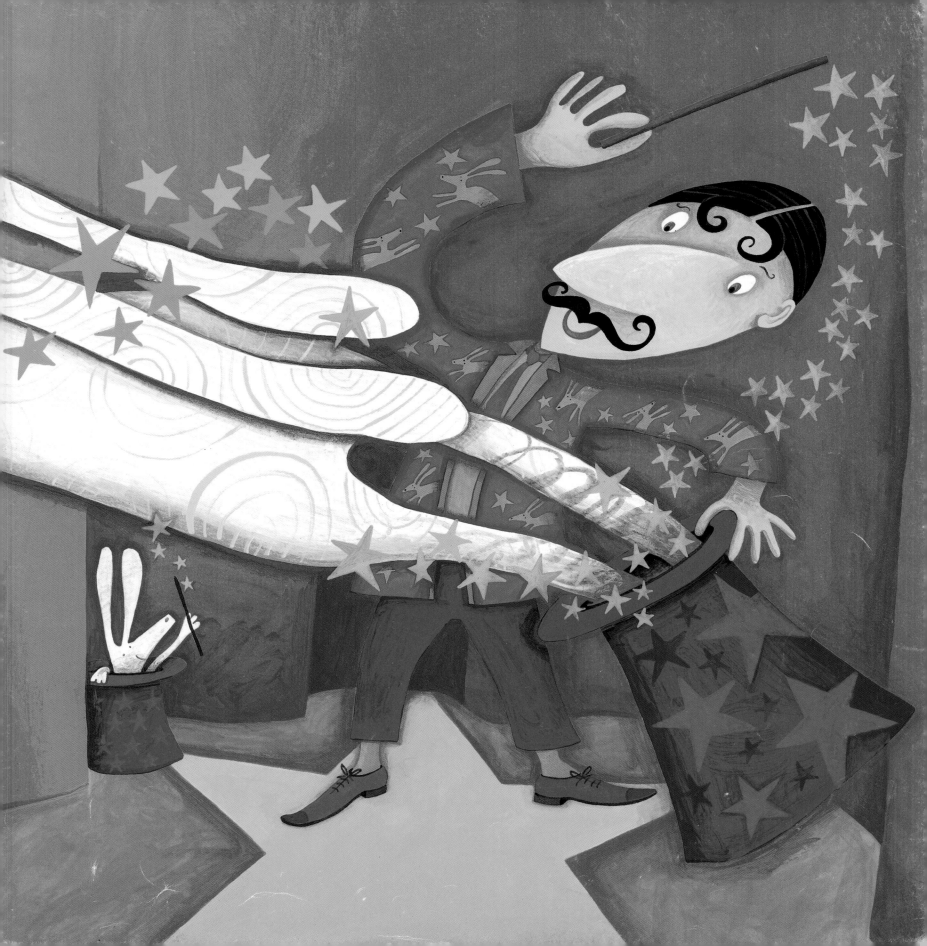

John Chapman had a hat.
They say he wore a cooking pot.
Some folks believe that, some do not.
If true—he was a sight indeed—
a pot-topped sower of apple seed.

Do **YOU** have a hat?

Amelia Earhart had a hat.
So did Daniel Boone—it's true.
Charlie Chaplin, Sally Ride . . .
all of them had hats.

Do **YOU**?

Do **YOU** have a hat?

A fancy hat? A hat that's plain?
A hat for walking in the rain?

A hat with feathers? Flowers? Bows?
A hat that hoots? A hat that glows?
A magic hat? A cap? A crown?
A country hat? A hat for town?

A single hat squashed flat . . . or tall . . .

is better than no hat at all!

Actor **Charlie Chaplin** was known for his endearing comic character "the tramp." The tramp wore a coat that was too small, pants that were too big, and a battered derby hat.

Igor Stravinsky was a Russian-American composer. He was best known for his ballets.

Amelia Earhart, born in 1897, was a well-known American aviator. She became the first woman to fly solo across the Atlantic Ocean.

Nat Love was born a slave. At age fifteen he left home to work as a cowboy near Dodge City, Kansas.